among = entire

Once Upon a

Bedtime

written by big people,
loved by little people

GW00802356

Illustrated by
Derry Dillon

This novel is entirely a work of fiction. The names,
characters and incidents portrayed in it are the work of the
author's imagination. Any resemblance to actual persons,
living or dead, events or localities is entirely coincidental.

Published 2014
by Poolbeg Press Ltd
123 Grange Hill, Baldoyle
Dublin 13, Ireland
E-mail: poolbeg@poolbeg.com

© Poolbeg Press 2014

The moral right of the author has been asserted.

Typesetting, layout, design, ebook © Poolbeg Press Ltd.

1

A catalogue record for this book is available from the British Library.

ISBN 978-1-78199-963-9

Typeset and illustrated by Derry Dillon

Printed by CPI Cox & Wyman, UK

This book belongs to

Hannah Patton

This is me with my family

INTRODUCTION

[handwritten: 1997] *[handwritten: BR]*

In 1997 Jonathan and his wife Senator Mary Ann O'Brien – Founder of Lily O'Brien's – set up the Jack & Jill Foundation, based on their own personal experience with their son Jack who died at home that year aged 22 months. His homecare plan became the blueprint for the foundation set up in his name.

Since then, the Jack & Jill Foundation has supported over 1,700 children with a unique service that includes financing of practical home nursing care, home visits by one of its liaison nurses, practical advice on caring for the child, listening to the family and making representations on their behalf to the government and HSE. Jack & Jill, spearheaded by Jonathan's relentless fundraising ability, has raised over €47 million since 1997 while only receiving €4.5 million from the State.

Jonathan has won many awards over the years including People of the Year, Global Fundraiser and, most recently, his work was recognised by the Royal College of Physicians of Ireland when he was conferred as their first and only Honorary Fellow of the Faculty of Paediatrics from a non-medical background.

We wish to thank all at *The RTÉ Guide*, Poolbeg, and all the authors and readers so much for their kind support from the sale of this book.

Jonathan Irwin

Jonathan Irwin,
Founder & CEO, Jack & Jill Foundation

CONTENTS

About the Author

Ger Duff

Ger Duff works in the public service and lives in Naas, County Kildare, with his wife, six-and-a-half-year-old daughter (that half is very important) and a pet kitten called Dubhín. He has been an aspiring scribbler (he says) since the age of seven but (knowing him) this could be yet another fairy tale.

How the Story Came About

*The inspiration for **A Silly Story** came from nowhere, literally. I had been attempting to edit one of my existing bedtime stories down to five hundred words (for this Poolbeg competition) but without success – it just wasn't working. Okay, Plan B – I'll write a new one. But that wasn't working either. And then, out of nowhere, the first line just popped into my head fully formed. This has happened before. Some might call it worrying but I call it lucky. And, as it transpired, in this case I was right.*

A Silly Story
by Ger Duff

"Cock-a-doodle-too-wit-too-whoo-doo," yelled Macalla the Wise Old Owl from the top of the purple barn early one morning.

1

"Sorry, could you say that again, please?" asked Duncan the One-Eared Donkey.

"Cock-a-doodle-too-wit-too-whoo-doo!" yelled Macalla.

"Yeah, that's what I thought you said," admitted Duncan. "But I wasn't too sure 'cos I only have one ear. So why did you say it?"

"Because I'm a rooster, of course," said Macalla. gal o

"No, Macalla. If you look in a mirror I think you'll find that you're an owl. In fact, I'm sure of it."

"No, no, dear one-eared Duncan, I am most definitely a rooster."

"Ahoy there, Oinky Pig!" called Duncan.

"Leave me alone," grumped Oinky. "I'm havin' me mornin' mud bath."

"Well, stop it for a moment and tell Macalla he's an owl," ordered Duncan.

"Meeoww!" said Oinky.

"What?" asked Duncan.

"I said meeoww!" repeated Oinky.

"Why?" demanded Duncan.

"Because I'm a kitty-cat," said Oinky.

"But you're a pig."

"No, I'm a kitty-cat. Listen – meeoww, purrrrr!"

"Has everyone gone mad?" shouted Duncan. "Hey, you, Fergie the Fearful Fox!"

"Ah, don't be botherin' me," growled Fergie. "I'm busy – I must go and count chickens in the chicken house."

"First, leave the chickens alone," ordered Duncan. "And second, tell Macalla that he's an owl and Oinky that he's a pig."

"Mooo!" said Fergie.

"Okay, okay, don't tell me," said Duncan. "Let me guess. You're a cow."

"Don't be silly," said Fergie.
"Of course I'm not a cow."

"At last," sighed Duncan.
"Someone with a bit of sense."

"No," laughed Fergie. "I'm
not a cow. I'm a bull. Mooo!
Mooo!"

"Oh, good grief," groaned Duncan. "Am I the only one left who can tell who is who on the farm?"

"No, I can tell who is who," said Robert the Rhubarb-Eating Rabbit.

"Can you? Can you really?" asked Duncan.

"Of course I can," replied Robert. "Macalla is a rooster, Oinky is a kitty-cat, Fergie is a bull and . . ."

"And what?" asked Duncan fearfully.

"And I am a green-and-orange wriggly worm," added Robert.

Duncan tapped his left front hoof impatiently.

"Why are you tapping your hoof impatiently?" asked Robert.

"Because I'm fed up waiting," said Duncan.

"For what?"

"For you to make a green-and-orange wriggly worm sound!"

"Ha ha, you silly donkey!" said Robert. "Worms don't make any sound. Everybody knows that."

11

"Oh yeah. Sorry, I forgot," admitted Duncan. "But that's because you all have me confused and mixed up with your messing about."

"Who's messing about?"

"All of you with your 'I'm a rooster' and 'I'm a kitty-cat' and 'I'm a bull' and 'I'm a wriggly worm' when I know that you're not!"

"You know?" said Robert. "I don't think so. Ha, I bet you don't even know what day it is."

"Oh yes, I do. It's Tuesday," said Duncan.

"No, it's April Fools' Day, you silly donkey! APRIL FOOL, DUNCAN!"

About the Author

Gwen Loughman

Gwen Loughman was a fixture behind many office desks before going on maternity leave to become a stay-at-home mother to four boy children, one Mister Husband and a dog – and is currently trying not to sweat the small stuff. She is from Athy, Co Kildare.

How the Story Came About

Declan was created purely by chance but he turned into a wonderful opportunity to show my sons how very few things are truly insurmountable; there is always a way around something. Sometimes kids can't see the forest for the trees so I used Declan as a means to an end – have a look at the problem, try a solution, watch the result and if it doesn't work, try again. I feel it is important to realise that everyone, regardless of who they are or what they look like, will meet obstacles at some stage in their life.

Declan the Fire-Breathing Dragon

I would like you to meet Declan the Fire-Breathing Dragon. He's not very big but he's the perfect size for his shape.

He's purple with green spikes running down his back and along his tail, and he has blue wings. He looks great!

But when Declan was younger
he was not your average fire-
breathing dragon. Firstly, he
was still learning how to breathe
fire. He found it a bit difficult
and tiring. Sometimes he made
huge flames and other times he

made tiny ones. And sometimes
he made huge flames when he
wanted tiny ones and tiny ones
when he wanted to make huge
ones. Declan practised very hard
to get it right even though it could
be quite frustrating. It also used
up a lot of energy.

Another interesting fact about Declan was that he was a vegetarian. This means he didn't eat meat. Vegetarian dragons are very rare creatures altogether. Especially purple-and-green ones.

Declan liked vegetables. Especially roasted ones, like carrots, onions, sweet potatoes and butternut squash.

For a treat Declan ate marshmallows. Except sometimes he burned them when he made the huge flames. But he ate them anyway!

Declan also liked ice cream. He really, really, REALLY liked ice cream.

It was probably his most favourite food in the world ever!

But Declan had a small problem. Every time he tried to eat ice cream (after he finished his roast vegetables!) he got SO excited he made way too much fire.

Huge flames shot out and melted his yummy dessert.

No matter how hard he tried he couldn't quite make tiny flames when he wanted to. In fact, he just couldn't stop making flames all the time – huge flames AND tiny ones.

It was a real dilemma because Declan didn't like warm, melted ice cream.

"I may as well eat soup!" he said, breathing out a tiny flame because he was so fed up. "Warm vanilla soup. Yuk!"

Declan had a human best friend called Iarla who wasn't purple and green. He had blue eyes and blond hair. Iarla didn't like to see Declan so upset, especially as he always ate all of his vegetables.

"I know!" Iarla jumped up and down in excitement. "Have a drink of water. It might put out your huge flames! Then you can eat your ice cream."

"But what if it works?" Declan was worried. "How will I get my flames back?"

Iarla had the answer again. "A minty sweet!" He was delighted with himself. "Eat a really hot minty sweet afterwards!"

Declan wasn't sure. But he really, really, REALLY wanted some ice cream so he took a big huge sip of water from the river.

And guess what? It worked!

It really did. The water put out both Declan's huge and tiny flames so he was finally able to enjoy his dessert.

He was so happy. The minty-sweet trick worked too and Declan was able to breathe his fire again, both huge and tiny flames.

And after a while he became so good at breathing fire he didn't need to sip water from the river or eat minty sweets any more.

25

About the Author

Susan Colgan

Susan Colgan lives in Dublin with her husband and three grown-up children. She has two dogs (Jake – who's adorable and very well-behaved . . . and Lexie – who's extremely adorable but a little minx), six buttonquails and a very nosy little robin who follows her about when she's pottering in the garden. She is currently writing a chick-lit novel. (Watch this space!)

How the Story Came About

I have always dabbled in writing, be it short stories, children's stories, poetry or attempting novels. I believe my writing was the natural progression of voracious reading activity in childhood. My nose was always stuck in some book or other, so when I found out that my Christmas story for the Jack & Jill Foundation had been accepted, it was lovely to know that I had participated (even if just a teenchy bit) in creating something which brought me so much pleasure as a child, for such a worthy cause.

It's Lonely at the Top

"Be careful, Mum!" said Holly, as she watched her mother climb the ladder to place Angelina the Angel on top of the Christmas tree.

"There!" said Mum, stepping down. "All done."

"Ooh, it's lovely!" said Holly, turning to Sam her younger brother. "Look at Ange . . . Sam! Stop picking your nose. It's disgusting!"

Sam wiggled a finger with something horrible and slimy on

top. "Want some?"

"Eeeuugh!" said Holly, running away, tripping over poor Lexie the dog who had been sleeping peacefully.

"Settle down, please, children!" said Mum. "Now, let's go leave out some cookies and milk for Santa."

"Don't forget a carrot for Rudolf!" said Sam.

Mum nodded. "And then it's time for bed!"

"Awww!" groaned the children as they all left the room.

Later that night, the Christmas tree began to rustle and shake.

"Do you think they're asleep yet?" a voice whispered.

"Yes, I can hear them snoring," someone giggled.

The tree rustled again as, one by one, all the ornaments on the tree began to move. First the snowman, followed by the sad, one-legged gingerbread man (Lexie had one time mistaken him for the kind you could eat). Then the ice-skater and the robin. Then all the others.

Soon the whole tree was alive.

"You look beautiful, Angelina," said the ice-skater.

"I know," she said, smiling down proudly.

"Would you like to come down and join us?" asked the ice-skater.

"Certainly not. I'm much too important for that!"

"I wish I could be an angel!" sighed the gingerbread man.

Angelina watched as all the Christmas figures played and chatted and laughed together. They were having great fun.

Suddenly, there was a strange creaking sound.

"Quick, everyone!" whistled the robin. "The ladder is falling! Grab onto a branch and hold on tightly!"

"Whaaaam!" The ladder fell onto the tree but it stayed standing. The decorations swung from side to side but eventually came to a stop.

"Is everyone okay?" whistled the robin, as he flew around the tree.

"Help!"

"Who's that?" the robin asked.

"It's me. Angelina. I've fallen to the bottom!"

"Don't worry. We'll help you get back up to the top."

"Will you really? That's very nice of you."

The ornaments all joined together in one big line down the centre of the tree.

"Okay," said the robin. "Start climbing."

Angelina started to climb.

Up she climbed. Higher and higher.

"So sorry," she said as she stood on people's feet and heads.

She was almost back to the top when suddenly she stopped.

"What's wrong?" asked the snowman.

"I don't think I want to be on the top anymore," she said. "It's much nicer to have friends. It's quite lonely at the top, you know."

"Well, stay with us then," said the snowman.

"But what about . . . ?"

The robin winked. "We'll think of something."

"Wow, look, Mum!" said Holly the next morning.

Perching proudly in Angelina's place at the top of the tree was the gingerbread man, grinning from ear to ear.

"My goodness!" said Mum, laughing. "Now that really does take the biscuit!"

About the Author

Sally Dillon

Sally Dillon is originally from Edinburgh. After many years in the catering industry she is now a full-time mum and carer to her sixteen-year-old son. She paints watercolours and writes when time permits. Sally can often be seen in North County Dublin walking her son's assistance dog. Say hello if you see her!

How the Story Came About

Stories always were, and are, very important in my house. The average amount of sleep, until my son reached fourteen, was four hours a night. We ran out of books, so I wrote my own. I always wrote gentle, happy stories with high visual impact, so we'd go to sleep with happy thoughts. The Jack & Jill Foundation helped me a lot when my son was a baby, so I am delighted that in some small way I've been able to help them.

If I Were a Cat

If I were a cat,
I'd much rather be,
Swimming in custard
Than climbing a tree.

I'd skip to the beach,
But when it got hot,
I'd go and cool off
On a millionaire's yacht.

If I were a cat,
And this just for fun,
I'd not howl at the moon
But miaow at the sun.

I'd drive a big bus
That was bright pink and red,
And give all the passengers
Tea in my shed.

If I were a cat
I'd sing in the shower,
Wear smart yellow wellies
And wash with a flower.

I'd climb on a cloud,
With a gold pogo-stick,
And I'd jump up and down
Until I felt sick.

But, as a mouse,
Thankful I'll be,
To see that yon cat
Is asleep on your knee.

About the Author

Kieran Marsh and Lesa Mirolo

Kieran Marsh works as an IT manager with a US multinational, managing a team that stretches from Chennai to Kansas. Lesa Mirolo studied art in Central St Martins, London, and is now teaching art and crafts to children full time. They are both from Dublin and reside there now, but were living in London when this piece was written.

How the Story Came About

Our first child, Brendan, was born twenty-one years ago. Inspired by the overwhelming joy of a new life, we put our creative hats on one weekend and put together a picture book, printed out on our noisy dot-matrix printer then richly illustrated by Lesa. It was a favourite of Brendan's, and later of his sisters', but then languished on the bookshelf for many years, unloved. We've now pulled out the story and freshened it up, in the hope that it might bring joy to a new generation.

Green

Once upon a very strange place indeed, lived a huge dragon named Green.

Green had great teeth and enormous talons, scales the size of dustbin lids and a tail as long as a whole crocodile. He could hold ten humans in his mouth if he wanted. Which he never did, because he liked people. He liked all kinds of people. Except maidens. For some reason, he just didn't like maidens.

He lived near a charming little mountain village, and he tried to help the villagers with everything. Unfortunately, he wasn't very good at helping. He had a habit of breaking things with his fierce talons or his great teeth, or accidentally setting fire to stuff with his extraordinarily spumous flame. But the village folk didn't mind. They baked him huge pies and had wonderful parties to thank him.

49

One day, Green's cousin Red from Normalsville came to visit. They looked very alike, except that Green was green and Red was red. However, Red was a dragon of the old school, fierce and human-hating. But, whenever he tried to attack the village, Green held him back. Even when he managed to swallow villagers, Green would make him vomit them up again.

One night, Red painted himself green and went to the village.

"Ho, Green!" cried the villagers. "Have you come for pie?"

"No," said Red. "I have come to eat you all! Ha ha ha!"

Red sprayed the village with flame, ate several farmers, and bit a young maiden clean in two.

The next day, the villagers took up their pitchforks and torches and sharp, pointy sticks and went to see Green.

"Ho, villagers!" called Green. "Have you come to give me pie?"

"No," said the villagers, "we have come to poke you with our pitchforks and torches and sharp, pointy sticks."

"But, what have I done?"

"You burnt our village."

"I never!"

"And ate some farmers."

"Certainly not."

"And bit a maiden clean in two."

"But, I don't like maidens. You

know I always stay well away from them."

The villagers stopped. "He's right," they said. "He's never been one for the maidens."

"Listen," said Green, "I think I know what's happening, and I have a plan."

That night, a green-painted Red turned up again at the village, expecting a fight, but this time the village was empty.

He had taken a deep breath, preparing his fire, when the roof of the church lifted. Green's head appeared, and he scorched Red with flame in a spumous flash.

Now, the fire did not hurt Red, but it burnt off all the green paint.

"Hey," said the villagers, "it was Red all along!"

So they poked him with their pitchforks and torches and sharp, pointy sticks until all Red's scales fell off. He looked really silly.

From that day on, Red could never fight humans, since he was too embarrassed by their laughter.

Green and the villagers had an especially big party with especially big pies. And no maidens!

About the Author

Aedín Collins

Aedín Collins is an aspiring author living in the West of Ireland with her French partner and their two *petites mademoiselles*. She blogs about parenting, lifestyle and raising a child with special needs.

How the Story Came About

As a mother of a child with Down syndrome, I am always on the look-out for stories that promote inclusivity and celebrate diversity. One night when I was putting Róisín to bed, I was struck by the ladybirds on her pyjamas. Ladybirds have such distinctive features and it got me wondering how would a ladybird whose spots were the wrong way round be treated – and so the tale of Larry the Ladybird was born.

60

Larry the Ladybird

There once was a field of beautiful yellow daffodils. Underneath the tallest daffodil lived a small village of ladybirds.

In that village lived a ladybird called Larry. He wasn't red like the other ladybirds. He was a black ladybird with red spots. The other ladybirds teased him and called him Mister Wrong Way Round.

Now, as you may not know, ladybirds love to dance. They have lots of legs, which make them quite good at it. The first dance of the summer was approaching, and Larry wanted to ask Lottie Ladybird to go with him but he was afraid she would say no on account of his spots being the wrong colour.

I know, thought Larry. I'll go to see the Emerald Fairy, who lives in the Enchanted Forest. She can cast a spell with her magic wand and my spots will be just like everyone else's.

In order to get to the Emerald Fairy, Larry would have to go through the valley of Ten Thousand Poppies, travel over Cherry Blossom Bridge and climb Cotton Candy Mountain.

Luckily, Larry could fly faster than all the other ladybirds but it was still a long way to go.

"I had better get started," said Larry.

He hadn't gone far when he heard a terrible commotion behind him. He flew back as fast as his little wings would carry him. When he got there, he couldn't believe his eyes! A bird had broken through the daffodil wall and was attacking the village!

He stood rooted to the spot, watching as the bird, a big fat crow, advanced on a few ladybirds, including Lottie.

Then Larry sprang into action. He threw himself in front of the crow, stuck his tongue out at him and shouted: "Hey, you big ugly bird, this way!"

The crow looked at Larry curiously – a black ladybird with red spots. He wondered if it would taste as nice as the red ladybirds. He decided to find out.

Larry flew as fast as his little wings would carry him. He led the crow higher and higher above the daffodils and away from the village. He swooped and circled and then climbed straight up towards the shining sun. The sunlight glinted on his red spots, causing them to sparkle like rubies. The sparkle blinded the crow, who could no longer see where he was going, and crashed into a branch of the old oak tree.

Dazed and embarrassed, the crow flew off. He would have to find lunch somewhere else.

Larry returned to the village where all the other ladybirds were cheering and celebrating.

"You saved us, Larry!" they cried.

"You and your amazing spots! We are sorry we teased you – please don't change them – we think they're wonderful!"

"Lottie, do you like my spots?" asked Larry.

"Of course! I've always loved your spots, Larry," said Lottie. "Will you go to the dance with me?"

"Yes!" cried Larry happily and then he and Lottie and all the other ladybirds danced and sang all night long.

About the Author

Fergus Dennehy

Fergus Dennehy is a recently graduated primary teacher out of Mary Immaculate College, Limerick. Born in Cork, he has lived in Tralee all of his twenty-three years. He balances most of his real life by living a dreamer lifestyle inside his head, which provides the inspiration for most of his stories. He has dreams of full-time professional writing.

How the Story Came About

Having read a lot of 'Big Books' as part of my teacher training, I felt that I had the right idea of the formula required to write an enjoyable story for children. I've always loved writing anyway, so this competition was the perfect chance to write something for a worthy cause such as the Jack & Jill Foundation. The 'lazy' of the story comes from pretty much how I was feeling the day I wrote it! Hope you enjoy! :)

Lester the Lazy Elf

This is a story about an elf. An elf named Lester.

Lester the Elf was a very lazy and sleepy person, preferring the comfort of his big blue bed and his big green slippers to

any sort of work or effort. He
liked his bed SO much, that he
even tried to buy a second big
blue bed for his office but he
wasn't allowed.

He would ROLL out of bed
in the morning, CRAWL on the
floor and SHUFFLE his feet all
the way to work.

You see, Lester, the very lazy elf, was actually one of Santa's elves and this meant that he never got to be as lazy and as sleepy as often as he would have liked.

Working with Santa was a very busy job, especially at Christmas time. His workshop was filled with THOUSANDS of elves running this way and that way across the HUGE wooden floor, carrying big presents and little presents, square presents and round presents, pointy presents and dull presents and my presents and your presents.

78

Lester HATED all this work. He would ROLL into the workshop, CRAWL towards the presents and SHUFFLE his feet all day as he carried only the smallest and easiest presents.

Santa and the other elves were not impressed with this laziness. One day, Santa had had enough.

"LESTER! If you don't stop being so lazy, I'm going to THROW you out of the North Pole!"

Lester was very worried and scared. He didn't know what he could do about his laziness. He had ALWAYS been lazy.

He decided to take a nap. He put on his big green slippers and hopped into his big blue bed and soon fell fast asleep.

Now, you mightn't know this about elves, but out of all the people in the world they have the biggest dreams. Lester was soon dreaming the biggest dream he'd ever had.

He was working in the workshop, late at night. It was VERY dark and he could hear all sorts of different sounds. He heard the CREAK-CREEEAK of the floorboards, the HOWLING of the wind and the PITTER-PATTER of the rain on the windows. He felt very nervous. He looked ALL around him but he could see nothing.

83

SUDDENLY . . .

He saw the shadow of a HUGE and MASSIVE MONSTER . . . coming towards him! Claws the size of the biggest presents and eyes the size of the pointiest!

Lester screamed the loudest scream! "HEELLLPPP!"

He could not run away – he could only ROLL, CRAWL and SHUFFLE! It had been so long since he moved quickly that his legs did not work anymore! He looked back . . . the monster was

*stomping closer and closer . . . his
claws were about to catch him . . .*

BOOM!

Lester woke in his bed with a scream and a bump. He was shaking and sweating all over. HE PROMISED HE WOULD NEVER BE LAZY AGAIN!

Today, Lester is the best Elf in the whole workshop. He carries ALL the big presents and ALL the pointy ones. He even RUNS to help others too!

About the Author

Kathleen Mc Causland

Kathleen Mc Causland comes from the picturesque village of Donaghmore in Co Tyrone. She has seven children, six grandchildren and has worked in Donaghmore Primary School for many years. Her love for children has been her inspiration to write and she enjoys writing stories for all ages from magical fantasy to comedy adventures. She's just a big kid at heart!

How the Story Came About

I've always enjoyed telling bedtime stories to my children, and now my grandchildren, on subjects from leprechauns to snowmen and everything in between! My inspiration for **Mister Moon, Light Up My Room!** *came one night when I was tucking my grandson Joshua into bed and he was afraid of the dark. 'Joshy' was letting his imagination work overtime so, as it was a bright moonlit night, I opened the curtains and said: "Mister Moon will light up your room." And so, the story was born! I'd like to dedicate it to Joshy and to my other five grandchildren Hannah-Kate, Harry, Eva, Anthony and Matilda.*

Mister Moon, Light Up My Room!

Joshy's bedroom was dark.

He felt scared.

He hid under his duvet.

Little by little he peeped out, slower than a slithering snail.

His eyes opened wide when he saw a tall, blue thing standing at his door!

"I wish I didn't see a big, blue giant with no face, no hands and no legs!" Joshy whispered.

Just then the moon peeped through his window.

The Man in the Moon smiled at Joshy and lit up his room as bright as day.

"Silly me, it's only my bathrobe hanging on the door," Joshy laughed.

The moon disappeared behind a fluffy-lamb cloud.

In a dark corner of his room, Joshy spied two shadowy shapes.

"Come back, Mister Moon! Light up my room! I see two greedy monkeys guzzling bananas! They're coming to gobble me up!" Joshy hollered.

The moon spun down like a gigantic yo-yo!

PLOP! PLOP! Out from the moon popped two golden arms!

PLOP! PLOP! Out popped two golden hands!

He plucked twinkling stars from the black sky.

He took a deep breath and his yellow cheeks grew fatter and fatter.

With one mighty WHOOSH he blew the stars into Joshy's room. The fiery stars fizzled and sizzled and burst wide open!

Magically, his room lit up!

"Silly me, it's only two dolls,

sucking their bottles," Joshy
giggled.

Joshy's room went dark –
again!

He saw a very peculiar animal
glaring at him!

"I wish I didn't see a hairy
monster with one black eye,
two white horns and white, sharp
teeth!" Joshy yelled. "Come back,

Mister Moon! Light up my room!"

The moon spun around in the sky.

PLOP! PLOP! Out from the moon popped two golden legs!

PLOP! PLOP! Out popped two golden feet!

He danced around the sky and plucked lots more dazzling stars.

He took a deep breath, and his

yellow cheeks grew fatter and fatter.

With one mighty WHOOSH he blew the stars into Joshy's room.

The fiery stars fizzled and sizzled and burst wide open!

The room lit up and in a flash the hairy monster vanished!

"Silly me, it's only my rocking horse grinning at me," Joshy

chuckled.

Joshy's room grew dark – again.

His bedroom door opened with a CREEKY-CREEEEEK!

Joshy saw a creepy crawly creature coming towards him!

"I wish I didn't see an ugly, bugly bug with two tails on its head, a dribbly tongue and sharp, scratchy claws!" Joshy hollered.

"Please come back, Mister Moon!
Light up my room!"

Mister Moon's huge face appeared
at the window.

He stuck out his red tongue at
Joshy's scary sister.

She ran screaming out the door.

"That was cool, Mister Moon,"
Joshy sniggered.

The Man in the Moon felt tired.

Joshy felt tired.

"Night-night, Joshy."

The Man in the Moon yawned . . . long and slow.

"Night-night, Mister Moon."

Joshy yawned . . . long and slow.

Mister Moon and Joshy fell fast asleep.

About the Author

Gráinne McDermott

Gráinne McDermott is a former nurse who now works as a primary school teacher in Rush, Co Dublin. She is originally from Co Monaghan but now lives happily by the sea in Donabate, Co Dublin.

How the Story Came About

I have enjoyed creative writing since childhood. I've written many stories, poems and plays with my pupils over the years. Recently, with much wonderful encouragement from my friends and loved ones (You know who you are!), I decided to try and share my stories with a wider audience and thus **Izzy in a Tizzy** *was born. I'm a great admirer of the Jack & Jill Foundation and I'm delighted to be part of this wonderful fundraiser.*

Izzy in a Tizzy

Izzy the Witch is very sad,
As her memory is so bad.
Her sister asked her round to tea,
But there's a problem as you'll see.

"I thought I'd hung it on the clock,
Where oh where is my other sock?
I've searched in every crack and cranny –
Can you help this muddled granny?"

"I'll scream if one more minute passes,
And still I haven't found my glasses.
Without them I can't see too far,
Try to find them, my little star."

"Oh my, I am a silly goat,
Where have I gone and left my coat?
A little help would do the trick,
Could you help me find it quick?"

"Deary, deary, darn and drat,
Where have I put my pointy hat?
I've searched in every single nook,
Be a dear and take a look."

"I do believe I have a curse,
For now I cannot find my purse,
I am as dizzy as can be,
Could you take a look for me?"

"I really am a dopey hag,
Where have I left my shopping bag?
I think I might just have a fit,
If you can't help me look for it!"

"I've looked below and up above,
But I can't see my other glove.
I need to find it, don't you see?
As time is running out on me!"

"I only have one pair to choose,
I can't believe I've lost my shoes.
I brought them all the way from France,
Can you spot them by any chance?"

"I know I put it by the pond,
Alas, I cannot see my wand.
I'm not sure where I placed it here,
But I am guessing it's quite near."

"I stayed up half the night to bake,
But now I've lost the chocolate cake.
Show me that you really care,
Can you see it anywhere?"

"Oh no, I've looked in every room,
Where did I put my magic broom?
Perhaps I left it in the shed,
Please help before I lose my head."

"Oh, fiddlesticks and froggy spawn,
Now my silly keys are gone.
I really, really need those keys,
Try to find them, pretty please."

"I really need to check the date,
To be sure that I'm not running late.
Oh yes, I really think I'd better,
Where could I have left that letter?"

"Oh me! Oh my! It is a crime
That I have wasted all this time!
I do think that I should sit down,
For I have been a silly clown.

Ah! Rushing really has its cost,
For here's the letter that I lost,
I'm not going out to tea,
My sister said she'd visit me!"

About the Author

Paula Redmond

Paula Redmond is from Gorey, Co Wexford. She is an engineer with an MSc in Business and Management. As well as writing, she is interested in arts and various crafts. She is an animal lover so no surprise that they appear in her story.

How the Story Came About

I still love travelling by train. I think there is something magical about this form of transport: the sound, the sights, the tunnels and the sleep-inducing effect it has on both young and old alike. In my story I hope to capture the sense of excitement that children experience when going somewhere new for the first time – the different people or in this case animals and places they see – and how travel opens up a whole new world of experience for them, even if they go just a few miles up the road.

Moo's City Adventure

Once upon a moon there was a cow called Moo. She was a pretty black-and-white cow with long eyelashes and a long tail to swat off flies. Moo lived on Fred's Farm in a lush green valley. There were lots of animals on the farm: ducks, sheep, chickens and two donkeys called Hee-Haw and She-Haw.

Moo's mammy told Moo that she was taking her to the city on the train. Moo was very excited, as she had never been on a train before.

Moo and her mammy stood on the platform behind the white line. Moo looked up and down the tracks waiting for the train to come. When she heard the CHOO-CHOO of the train she let out a "MOO! MOO!" with excitement.

As they rolled through the countryside Moo gazed out the window. They passed through towns and villages, went over hills and under bridges. She saw children going to school, postmen delivering letters and fields full of fluffy sheep.

Suddenly everything went dark and Moo let out a scared "MOOOOOO!". Mammy Moo told her everything was okay, that they were just passing through a tunnel.

Moo couldn't believe how busy the city was. She was used to the quiet countryside.

BEEP! BEEP! The noise of cars scared her at first but she soon got used to them.

The tallest building on Fred's Farm was the bright red barn where all the animals snuggled up at night-time. The buildings in the city were much higher than Fred's barn and Moo got dizzy looking up.

The footpath was so busy with people that Moo had to hold on to her mammy's tail so she wouldn't get lost.

"Look at that cow, Mammy, she's red!" Moo said excitedly. "And look at that one – he's all black!"

Moo had only ever seen black-
and-white cows like her before.

"Yes," Mammy Moo said. "Cows come in lots of different colours.

Black and white,
Red or brown,
Four hooves and a tail,
All cows moo the same!"

Then Moo saw a black-and-green duck across the street. Her friend David Duck on the farm was brown-and-white. Moo didn't know ducks could be different colours.

"I thought all ducks were the same as David!" she said.

Mammy Moo replied:
"Black and green,
White or brown,
Two flippers and two wings
All ducks make the same sound,
QUACK! QUACK!"

As Moo gazed out the train window on the way home she thought about all of the things she had seen in the city. She couldn't wait to tell her friends – Shelly and Shane the sheep, Paul the pig and Hilda, Helen and Henrietta the hens, about all of the amazing sights.

She knew now that not every-thing was the same as on her farm and that there were lots of different-looking animals in the world.

As the train rolled along Moo's eyelids got heavy and her hooves ached from all of the walking she had done.

"I'm just going to rest my eyes," she said in a sleepy voice and dozed off to the CHOO-CHOO sound of the train.

About the Author

Marion O'Connor

Marion O'Connor works in Fáilte Ireland in Dublin. Originally from Galway and Roscommon, she currently lives outside of Athboy, Co Meath, with her husband James Corcoran and one-and-a-half-year-old daughter Sinéad.

How the Story Came About

My writing has been inspired by both my daughter Sinéad, who experiences wonder and excitement in the simplest of items, and my dad, who has written many quirky and enjoyable stories. My story in this collection is based on the fact that every child yearns for a best friend, be it real, imaginary or different. Seeing life through a child's eyes provides endless opportunities for fun and adventure!

My Best Pal Stevie

I have a best friend that nobody knows about. He is the most caring friend that anybody could wish for. He has a nicely shaped head and the sparkling green eyes of a cat. He wears glasses, has thin hairy legs, six at that, rosy cheeks and has a tiny-weeny little dot of a nose. Anyhow, that's Stevie – Stevie Spider – and we get on just great.

I can remember very clearly the first day we met. I was getting dressed for school and then suddenly he appeared from under my bed. I screamed. He screamed. Then we both screamed together.

His tiny suitcase went flying into the air and landed with a thud. What a mess! He asked if he could lodge in the wardrobe for a while as he was looking for a place to stay. From that day onwards he slept in my wardrobe and we became the best of friends.

At six o'clock in the morning I always get my morning call from Stevie. He gives me a little rub on my cheek with his silky legs and he delights in seeing my eyelids gradually open.

Stevie then taps his feet impatiently, waiting for his breakfast. Four sausages, three rashers, four black puddings and a bowl of Weetabix. Oh boy, has he an appetite!

We often get up to mischief, Stevie and me. Stevie came to school with me one day, hidden in my bag. I told him to stay quiet and to read his book. Do you think he did that? No, he didn't! Instead he jumped on my teacher Miss Laverty's head and danced on her curls. All of the class started to laugh but Miss Laverty didn't find it funny. She started to run around the room screaming for help. He wouldn't harm anyone but I told him not to do it again.

Another day he frightened poor Mrs Maguire next door by hiding in her jacket pocket. When she put her hand in she squealed and tried to hit him but Stevie was too fast for her.

Some days Stevie is gone out when I come home from school. He is often visiting his good spider friends, Barney and Sally. They live in the house next door – in the owner's shoes to be exact – Ugh!! At least a wardrobe is better than that, I say! They often have spider parties and stay up all night in their pyjamas, laughing and drinking lemonade. Spiders have a great life, you know.

Every night we do the same thing before going to bed. I brush my teeth and comb my hair but Stevie only has to comb his hair. Spiders have no teeth, you see!

We read each other a story before turning the light off.

"Night-night, Stevie," I say then.

He is already asleep. I can hear his snores.

He is my best friend and I his. Hopefully it will always stay that way.

About the Author

Grace Egan

I am a sixth-year student in Mercy Mounthawk Secondary School in Tralee, Co Kerry. I am seventeen years old. I live on a dairy farm in Ardfert with my mom, my older brother and sister, and lots of pets.

How the Story Came About

*I have always loved writing stories, ever since I was younger when I would imagine wild adventures for my toys to go on. When I saw the competition in the **RTÉ Guide**, to write a children's story, I had to enter. With the winning stories being published in time for Christmas, I wanted to create a main character in line with the festive season: a robin. Many children, and adults, can find it difficult to make friends, which is what inspired me to write a story for these children to relate to.*

Robbie the Robin Makes a Friend

Robbie the Robin lived in a tiny nest in a tall tree. Robbie had no one to play with in his tree and this made him very sad.

"Why don't you go outside and find someone to play with?" said Robbie's mom.

"Okay, Mom," replied Robbie and he flapped his wings and set out on his journey.

Some time later Robbie had been flying around the whole forest looking for a friend to play with him and his wings were getting tired. He was just about to give up when he saw Darragh Deer playing with his friends so he swooped down to talk to him.

"Can I play with you, Darragh?" asked Robbie.

"Sorry," said Darragh, "but you're too small to play with me and my friends because we're having a race."

Next Robbie flew over the lake looking for someone to play with him. He spotted Frankie Frog.

"Frankie will play with me," he said as he flew over to Frankie.

"Can I play with you, Frankie?" he asked.

"I'm sorry, Robbie, but my friends and I are going swimming and you can't swim," replied Frankie.

Robbie tried searching on the ground for some friends. Matilda Mouse was so small that he barely saw her at first. He was sure that Matilda would let him play with her because she couldn't say he was too small and she wouldn't be going swimming.

"Can I play with you, Matilda?" asked Robbie.

"You're too big to play with me, Robbie. I'm sorry," said Matilda.

Robbie Robin sat down on a rock and thought about what to do next. He was very upset because no one would play with him and he decided to fly home.

"This is a very prickly rock," he said then.

He hopped off the rock and was shocked to see that it was not a rock, but a hedgehog.

"Hello, I am Robbie Robin. What's your name?"

The spiky hedgehog looked at Robbie and whispered, "I am

Henry Hedgehog and no one likes to play with me because I'm too prickly."

Robbie had found a friend at last!

"I'll play with you!" shouted Robbie. "Let's play hide-and-seek. I can fly up to the trees and count to ten and you can hide in the leaves down here!" He was so happy!

Robbie Robin and Henry Hedgehog spent hours playing hide-and-seek. They were having so much fun that they didn't realise how much time had passed and Robbie's mom and Henry's mom had to call them home when it was bedtime.

When Robbie's mom was tucking him into his nest that night, she asked him if he was going to play outside again tomorrow.

"Yes," yawned a sleepy Robbie. "Henry's my best friend and I'm going to play with him every day."

About the Author

Veronica Casey

Veronica Casey is a communications teacher by profession, and currently runs literacy and creative writing courses for adults. As well as being a mum of four, her willing muses and toughest critics when it comes to writing children's stories, she also runs her own pre-school. She spends whatever time she can writing stories and poetry for both children and adults alike.

How the Story Came About

*The idea for **Nick's Nightmares** came from a chat my kids were having while tidying up. They were wondering what they would do if the bad things in nightmares were to come true. This led to them talking about objects, like the Hoover, coming to life and how they would bravely defeat these objects. Needless to say there was a lot more chat than cleaning done, but the seeds for the story were sown.*

Nick's Nightmares

"I want to be a footballer!" Nick says.
"Oh no!" sighs Dad, scratching his head.

Nick plays in the rain.
He jumps and he ducks.
He kicks the ball high
And rolls in the muck!

But there's mud on the sofa,
Mud on the mat,
Mud down the hallway,
And mud on the cat!

"What a nightmare, Nick!" says Dad.
"Clean that mess up, quick, quick, quick!"
Silly Dad, don't you know,
I want to be a footballer when I grow.

"I want to be a painter!" Nick says.
"Oh no!" sighs Dad, scratching his head.

Nick mixes his colours.
He draws big brown mice.
He paints great green giants,
And brightest blue skies.

But there's paint on the ceiling,
Paint on his head,
Paint on the windows,
And paint on his bed!

"What a nightmare, Nick!" says Dad.
"Clean that mess up, quick, quick, quick!"
Silly Dad, don't you know,
I want to be a painter when I grow.

"I want to be a builder!" Nick says.
"Oh no!" sighs Dad, scratching his head.

Nick builds great tall towers.
He knocks them back down.
He makes rocky roads,
And zooms cars around.

But there are bricks in the laundry,

Bricks on the chairs,

Bricks in the oven,

And bricks on the stairs!

"What a nightmare, Nick!" says Dad.

"Clean that mess up, quick, quick, quick!"

Silly Dad, don't you know,

I want to be a builder when I grow.

"I want to be a hero!" Nick says.

"Oh no!" sighs Dad,

scratching his head.

Nick plays a pirate prince.

He is the bravest fireman.

He becomes a super soldier,

And a spy with a secret plan.

But there are clothes on the landing,
Clothes on the floors,
Clothes on the bannisters,
And clothes behind doors.

"What a nightmare, Nick!" says Dad.
"Clean that mess up, quick, quick, quick!"
Silly Dad, don't you know,
I want to be a hero when I grow.

Soon day turns into night-time.
"I want to go to sleep!" Nick says.
"Oh thank goodness!" sighs his dad,
And he puts Nick straight to bed.

Nick closes his eyes and dreams . . .

That he is a pirate princess!

Who slips on the muddiest mess!

Who gets chased by footballs,

Down the stairs, through dark halls.

Then into the laundry headfirst
Nick goes,
Where a polka-dot paintbrush
tickles his toes.
And a monster mouse with his
hands on his hips,
Shouts aloud, "I told you to clean
up all this!"

"I should have cleaned it up!"

Nick screams

As Dad wakes him gently from his dreams.

He says, "It's just a nightmare, Nick!

Go back to sleep now, quick, quick, quick!"

Nick closes his eyes, but before he sleeps,
He makes a promise he hopes to keep.
"Thank you, Dad, you are the best.
I promise now to clean up my mess."

"That would be a dream come true!"
Dad says,
Tucking Nick safely back into bed.
"Let's hope you remember in the morning.
Nighty night, my sleepyhead!"

159

About the Author

Aodhbha Schüttke

Aodhbha Schüttke lives in Clontarf with her family and she is currently starting her final year studying medicine in Trinity College Dublin. She has always enjoyed writing in her spare time, and has already written, as yet unpublished, a series of four children's fantasy novels, the first of which she wrote when she was seventeen.

How the Story Came About

When I was studying medicine, we had a paediatrics module where every student was encouraged to bring a toy along with our usual equipment: stethoscope, pen, notes, watch. I had a bright-green frog, whom I named "Vincent". He came everywhere with me through the hospital and was popular with students and children alike. It was easy to imagine a personality and background for my toy helper and the children liked adding their own twists to his ever-growing stories. I also came in contact with the Jack & Jill Foundation during my studies, and am very much aware of their superb and invaluable work. I am honoured and delighted to be able to contribute to such a worthy cause with this publication.

The Flying Frog

In a garden there was a big pond.
Ducks swam above, fish swam
below, and in the middle frogs
sat on lily pads. There were green
frogs, blue frogs, stripy frogs, and
speckled frogs.

The greenest of all the frogs was called Vincent. Vincent sat on his lily pad in the sun, and looked up at the big blue sky.

Vincent said: "I wish that I could fly. If I had wings, I'd spread them out, and soar into the sky!"

"Why fly when you can swim or jump?" the other frogs croaked. "A frog could never fly!"

Vincent tried jumping very high. He tried running very fast before he jumped. He tried jumping again once he was in the air. But, every time, he fell back down onto his lily pad. The other frogs laughed.

Vincent hopped to the edge of the pond, to where the ducks' nests were. He looked around the twigs and eggs, collecting feathers in his arms.

"What are you doing beside our nests?" the ducks quacked.

"I'm collecting feathers to make me fly," Vincent said. "If I had wings, I'd spread them out, and soar into the sky!"

But the ducks did not trust the frog.

"Get away from our eggs before you break them!" they squawked. They flapped their wings, and nearly knocked poor Vincent over. He found a quiet corner by the pond. Using thread from a spider's web he tied the feathers together. Soon he had made wings to tie to his arms.

He flapped his new wings. He ran while he flapped. He jumped while he flapped. But, every time, he fell down to the ground.

Vincent climbed a reed hanging over the pond. The fish in the water watched.

"What are you doing up there, Vincent?" the fish gurgled.

"I'm going to try to fly. You see these wings? I'll spread them out, and soar into the sky!"

Taking a deep breath, he jumped and flapped his wings. But poor

Vincent fell with a splash into the pond. The fish all laughed.

Vincent swam to the edge of the pond. His wings were drenched with water. He took his wings off his arms. He sighed.

"It seems I'll never fly. Without real wings, I can't take off, and soar into the sky!"

"I have wings," a small voice trilled.

Vincent looked around. A wren was perched on a reed. It was his dear friend Frank.

"If you like, I'll help you learn to fly," said Frank.

Frank held Vincent's shoulders with his feet. Frank flapped his little wings.

Up and up they went, far above the pond. Vincent laughed and cheered and whooped as they soared through the sky.

Down by the pond the frogs all gawped, the ducks all stared and the fish all gasped. They were amazed to see Vincent flying.

"Thank you!" Vincent said when they landed. "That was very kind! You are a good friend!"

"I wonder," Frank began. "Could you teach me how to swim?"

About the Author

Veronica Roche

Veronica Roche grew up in Waterford, not far from its beautiful beaches, and they still are her favourite places. Upon finishing her studies at UCC, she went on to work for a large multinational company, specializing in languages. When she is not looking after her dogs, cats and turtles, she tries to keep tags on her three lovely girls.

How the Story Came About

To spread a little magic and make a little child smile.

The Little Magic Turtle

This is the story of the Little Magic Turtle.

Little Magic Turtle was very special. He lived in a secret magical place that only other Magic Turtles knew about. Every morning he woke up, crept out of his magic egg and said good morning to his friends on the silvery secret beach where he lived. There were starfish and shellfish, big crabs, little crabs and all kinds of other friendly fish from the blue, blue ocean. Every morning they all had breakfast together sitting on the sandy beach and then played lots of games, swimming and splashing in the woolly, white waves. Every evening, when they were all tired and hungry, they sat on the slippery stones and watched the golden sun sinking into the sparkling sea and had supper.

Yes, Little Magic Turtle lived a truly magical life.

And then, one morning, while they were playing hide-and-seek in the rock pools, Little Magic Turtle saw something glittering in the water of the pool where he wanted to hide. He looked a little closer – and then it was gone! Little Magic Turtle rubbed his eyes, blinked hard and looked again. There it was – a little silver streak flashed through the water and then disappeared.

Little Magic Turtle was a very curious little turtle, so he decided to investigate. He put on his magic swimming goggles and climbed over the rocks and into the pool. He looked here and there and almost everywhere, and then, just when he had almost given up (but only almost because magic turtles never give up), he saw two big sad eyes looking up at him from underneath a pink coral.

"Oh please, Little Turtle, please don't eat me!" cried a little tiny voice from a little tiny fish.

"Little Fish, of course I won't eat you! I am Little Magic Turtle – we can be friends."

Two big tears escaped from Little Fish's eyes. He was trying to be very brave, but he was very scared.

"Why are you crying, Little Fish? Don't you want to come and play with me and my friends? We'll have lots of fun!"

"I can't leave my little rock pool," said Little Fish in a sad little voice as two even bigger tears rolled down his cheeks. "I was playing hide-and-seek with my friends when a big, bouncy wave came in and all my friends went back out to sea with the wave. I was hiding under the pink coral and now the sea has gone. I can't walk on the sandy beach like you, Little Magic Turtle."

Little Magic Turtle thought for a moment. "Don't worry, Little Fish – I have an idea!"

Little Magic Turtle climbed up onto a rock and called out to his friends – and his magic egg! Suddenly Little Crab and Big Crab, all the starfish, shellfish, his magic egg and his other friends appeared. They talked for a little while, and then they filled Little Magic Turtle's magic egg with water and told Little Fish to jump in.

At first, Little Fish was scared,
but then, when they told him their
plan, he clapped his fins with glee.
"Oh, thank you, Little Magic
Turtle! That is a good plan!" And
in he jumped.

All the little starfish and big starfish joined together and made a spangly path down the beach from the rock pools to the sea. Then Little Crab and Big Crab rolled the Magic Egg carefully down the starfish path to the sea.

Little Magic Turtle bobbed about in the waves and, together with all his other friends, called out for Little Fish's friends to come and fetch him.

In a flash, Little Fish's friends darted to the shore.

"Little Fish! Where have you been? We were so worried!" they cried.

Little Fish was so happy to see his friends again he jumped for joy out of the magic egg and into the sea. And then they all swam around together as happy fish do.

"Thank you, Little Magic Turtle and all your friends for helping me," said Little Fish with a big happy smile.

Then, with a flick of their tails, all of the fish waved goodbye and swam out into the blue, blue ocean. Little Magic Turtle and all his friends stayed on the shore and waved back.

"See you soon, Little Fish. Come back and play tomorrow!" called Little Magic Turtle.

And then they all went home and

fell asleep and dreamt of bouncy waves and rock pools and what they would play tomorrow.

About the Author

Ciarán Hickey

Ciarán Hickey is a student filmmaker and writer living in Maynooth, Co Kildare, with his parents, younger sister and mischievous dog. He attends the National Film School in Dun Laoghaire and has directed multiple short films and the occasional stage play.

How the Story Came About

The Little Monster is a written adaptation of a short film written and directed by me as part of my college course. The no-dialogue film was selected to be made by IADT College lecturers. The short, titled Monster, was filmed in April of 2014 and is set to be released online for Christmas. It was my mother who suggested I turn my short film into a written children's story.

The Little Monster

Once upon a time there was a Little Monster who loved nothing more than to read stories before bed. He loved all sorts of stories, but his favourites by far were the scary ones – the ones his mum and dad said he shouldn't read because he would have nightmares and wouldn't be able to sleep.

And out of all the scary stories
he had read, he liked none better
than the story called *The Scary
Human Living Under the Bed*.

It was a particularly scary night when the Little Monster sat quivering in bed reading about the Scary Human, and how it loved nothing more than scaring little monsters like him. So scared was the Little Monster that when an owl flew past his window and let loose a shrill "Hoot!" he jumped in fright, dropping his book to the floor with a loud thump! But when he poked his head over the edge of the bed, his book was nowhere to be seen! Could it perhaps have fallen under the bed?

The Little Monster very nearly hid under the covers in fear at the thought of looking under his bed, certain the Scary Human would be there waiting. But he remembered how brave the heroes in his stories were and decided he must be brave now as well.

Peering under the bed, the Little Monster saw only darkness. No book. Getting down onto the floor to get a better look, he saw only more darkness. No book. Mustering up all his courage, he crawled under his bed, but still – no book. Coming out the other side, the Little Monster was very confused, not having found anything.

But wait – there! In front of him on the floor – his book! He pulled himself out from under the bed and grabbed it, holding it tight to him in glee.

But standing up, the Little Monster jumped in shock! This wasn't his room! Everything was different.

And asleep in the bed was . . . a human!

The Little Monster stepped back in terror as the human rolled over in its sleep. It was small, and not as scary as the pictures in his story. And at the foot of its bed was . . . a book just like the Little Monster's. He carefully picked it up and was shocked to see written there . . . *The Story of the Scary Monster!*

The Little Monster looked at the Little Human, and realised it was afraid of monsters just as he was afraid of humans. Putting the books down on the bed the Little Monster smiled and, forgetting his fear, tucked in the Little Human. The boy smiled and rolled over, a nightmare forgotten.

It was time for the Little Monster to go home, but as he crawled back under the bed, he left something behind him for the little human to have . . . his storybook, left open on the story of the Scary Human who loved to frighten Little Monsters.

197

About the Author

Jackie O'Shea

Jackie O'Shea is originally from Co Clare but now lives in Dublin with her husband Stephen, sons Alex and Seán, two goldfish and hundreds of dust bunnies.

How the Story Came About

When I began to write this bedtime story, I thought of what it would be like to be a child at night. I thought about the Jack & Jill children who mightn't feel well or understand what was happening around them. What was night-time like for them? I remembered when I was worried as a child – I would hear strange noises at night and imagined horrible, monstrous causes for them. So I thought I'd take this idea and turn it on its head – instead of scary noises, why not make them fun and magical? And who better for a guide than a bright star to lead the way through the darkness?

The Wandering Star

Alan was afraid of the dark. At night he jumped quickly into bed in case something under it reached out and grabbed his leg. He heard strange noises as he lay huddled under his quilt. He left his bedside light on all night.

But he was still afraid.

One night, Alan woke with a start. The light in his room was brighter than usual. He sat up and there, sitting on the windowsill, was a golden star.

"I am the Wandering Star," it said in a soft, tinkling voice. "I seek out children who are afraid of the dark and show them the world at night. Do you want to come and see?"

Alan gulped. He was frightened

but he was also curious. He nodded quickly. The Star twirled around and Alan found himself floating outside his window, holding the Star's hand.

"Off we go!" chuckled the Star, and it whisked Alan away, leaving a trail of twinkling light.

They flew over the rooftops.

Suddenly, Alan heard a flapping and a tapping.

"What's that?" he asked anxiously.

"Ah, look!" replied the Star.

Alan looked and saw a glittery shape on a nearby windowsill. At first, he thought it was a moth but, as they swooped down, he realised who it was.

"Hello, Alan," said the Tooth Fairy. "That was a lovely, shiny tooth you left me last week."

"Thank you for the coin,"

stuttered Alan, remembering his manners.

"You're welcome!" smiled the Tooth Fairy as she slipped through the open window.

On the Star went, with Alan clutching its hand tightly.

Soon they came to a wood and landed on a branch of a giant chestnut tree. Alan heard a rumbling and a rustling.

"What's that?" he asked nervously.

"Ah, listen!" said the Star.

As Alan listened, he realised that the great tree was chuckling as its branches swayed in the breeze.

"The wind is tickling the tree," whispered the Star.

The Star and Alan flew over the wood and down to the wide ocean. In the distance, Alan heard a splashing and a crashing.

"What's that?" he asked the Star wonderingly.

"Ah, see!" replied the Star.

Alan saw a dark-blue whale slowly rising from the water and then flipping backwards in a magnificent spray of silvery water.

"Amazing!" he gasped.

"Thank you!" boomed the whale and he disappeared under the waves.

"Home time!" giggled the Star and off they went, across the sea, through the wood, over the roof-tops until they arrived back at Alan's house.

"How do you feel now?" asked the Star.

"Not scared at all!" laughed Alan.

But then he had a thought.

"Star, does something live under my bed?" he asked warily.

"Have a look!" said the Star and, with a quiet pop, he disappeared.

Alan leaned over the edge of his bed and peeked underneath. There, hopping around in the shadows, he could see them: soft, grey and furry.

"Dust bunnies!" he laughed
and with that he turned off his
light and fell fast asleep.

About the Author

Bill Waverly

Bill Waverly is a native of Drogheda now living in Dublin. He is married with two children. As a child he loved to read and grew up surrounded by the likes of Tolkien, Dahl and CS Lewis. Bill has always loved to write, and always carries a notebook with him to jot down ideas. He loves to write stories for children, and he is very pleased and humbled to have been included in this collection of short stories for such a worthy cause.

How the Story Came About

*I have always loved to write, particularly children's stories, and had once planned to write a book called **The Tales of Roarke**, which was all about a little boy and girl who will not go to sleep at night. So a wise old bird called Roarke promises to visit them each night to tell them a bedtime story, after which they must agree to sleep!*

The story about the nightingale was to be the first of these tales. The Poolbeg competition was for such a good cause, it gave me the incentive to revisit the nightingale, and I hope that children everywhere (and perhaps a few adults) will like the story.

The Sun, the Moon and the Nightingale

Once upon a time, many many years ago, the Sun and the Moon started to fight about who owned the Earth.

"The Earth is mine!" bellowed the Sun as it hurled its hot rays at the Moon.

"No, it's mine!" roared the Moon as it reflected the rays onto the Earth.

The rays began to warm the Earth. The soil became very dry. There was no rain. Plants and animals grew very thirsty.

The creatures of the land and sea met to discuss what could be done. The cheetahs chattered. The rhinos roared. The whales wailed.

The fish fretted.

"Perhaps I have the answer," chirped the nightingale. "My singing will soothe the Sun and the Moon and stop them fighting."

"Brave nightingale!" said the eagles. "We will help you. We will carry you to the place where the Sky meets the Stars."

So the flock of eagles took turns to carry the nightingale towards the Moon first, as it was closer than the Sun.

The Moon was so busy arguing with the Sun that it didn't notice the small bird approach.

"Big hot bully!" it roared. "The earth belongs to me!"

The nightingale began to sing.

"What a wonderful song!" the Moon declared, forgetting the argument for a moment.

"Dear Moon," the nightingale said, "I will happily sing for you if you stop your fighting. Your battle with the Sun is causing our planet a lot of suffering."

"What?" the Moon roared. "Let that big greedy ball of fire think he has won? Never!"

So the nightingale flew towards the Sun.

"Dear Sun," said the nightingale, "I will sing for you forever if you will stop this war between you and the Moon."

"Let that big old ball of rock think he has won? Never!" roared the Sun.

With one last great effort, the tired and weak nightingale sang a song that was so sad that the rocks on the Moon broke in two, while the Sun itself cried tears of fire.

Then, exhausted, the poor bird fell back to Earth and was caught gently by one of the eagles.

Everything seemed to stop for a moment.

The lifeless nightingale was carried up to the top of the highest mountain where the Sun and Moon could see her.

"I am sorry, Moon!" cried the Sun.

"I am sorry too, Sun!" cried the Moon.

"How could we be so cruel?" they both cried. "Oh, the poor nightingale!"

Suddenly the nightingale opened her eyes.

The Moon and Sun cheered! The Sky wept tears of joy and its rain fell on the Earth to great shouts from all of the animals and plants.

From that day on the Sun and Moon agreed to share the Earth between them. The Sun took the day, and the Moon took the night and, as for the nightingale, well, as soon as she recovered, she suddenly . . . but wait . . . that is a story for the next time!

About the Author

Karen Quinn

Karen Quinn is an MA graduate in English from Queen's University Belfast. She is currently active as an actress, and as artistic director of QuothMe Productions, with whom she is currently producing and directing the filming of a collection of scenes from *Romeo and Juliet*, and *Macbeth*. Karen also enjoys painting, photography and playing the violin in her free time.

How the Story Came About

We all remember our favourite children's stories. We might not remember every detail, but we remember the important parts – the bits and pieces that we collect and take with us as we grow. They are usually lessons that help to shape us into the people we are today.

I love writing for children; they are our future writers, doctors and volunteers. They will find a cure for cancer and invent unimaginable and amazing things. So they are the inspiration behind this story. I'd like to say that I helped mould a great inventor, a brave doctor and a caring person. After all, Jack & Jill exists because of them.

The Little Owl

There once was a Little Owl who wore a red jumper. His mother knitted it for him because he was often cold.

He lived in the forest with lots of other owls. They were bigger and stronger and fluffier than him. They teased the Little Owl for being so small. They teased the Little Owl for wearing a red jumper. They also teased the Little Owl for not knowing how to hoot.

Mother Owl tried to teach him.
"Too-wit-too-whooooo!"
she would say.

"Twit," the Little Owl would respond.

Mother Owl would ruffle her feathers and try again: 'TOO-WIT-TOO-WHOOOOOO!'"

The Little Owl would think
and blink and think some more.
Then with all his might, he would
shout: "TWIT!"

The Little Owl tried and tried,
but he just could not hoot. He didn't
like to be different. Different
meant that he couldn't go on
adventures with the other owls.
Different meant that snow made
him feel cold. Most of all though,
different meant loneliness. The
Little Owl hated feeling lonely.

Maybe I'm not meant to be an owl, he thought. Maybe I'm meant to be a snail, or a skunk.

So the Little Owl flew deeper into the forest, past the big old oak, past the green-soaked swamp and towards the mighty evergreens.

There in the moonlight he saw an otter playing in a stream.

Maybe I'm meant to be an otter, he thought. So he landed on a rock beside him.

"*Squeak, squeak!*" said the otter.

"Twit!" said the Little Owl. The otter screwed up his nose.

Maybe the Little Owl wasn't an otter after all.

So the Little Owl flew deeper again, this time coming across a wood pigeon, nestled in a tree.

"*Coo-coo!*" said the wood pigeon.

"Twit!" said the Little Owl.

He was definitely not a wood pigeon.

Finally he flew towards the lake, where a big crocodile was sleeping in the reeds. The Little Owl landed on her head.

"Twit!" said the Little Owl.

"*Hisssss!*" said the crocodile.

He wasn't a crocodile – he was dinner!

The Little Owl flew to a nearby branch. He wanted to go home but was very, very lost. He cried, his teardrops glittering in the lake below.

The crocodile edged closer, the wood pigeon flew above his head and the otter rested by his feet.

"This little owl called me a twit!" said the crocodile.

"Me too," said the otter, "but he is lost, I think."

"Then we shall bring him home," said the wood pigeon.

So together they went through the deep forest, past the mighty evergreens, the green-soaked swamp and the big old oak.

The Little Owl was surprised to find all the owls looking for him. They chirped and danced when he returned.

Mother Owl covered him in lovely kisses.

The Little Owl was home. He also had three new friends. They didn't hoot – they cooed, hissed, and squeaked. Maybe being different wasn't bad at all, the Little Owl thought. Maybe being different is what made them special.

About the Author

Linda Kennedy

Linda Kennedy lives in Rathfarnham with her husband and three children. She worked in a clinical/medical supply company for many years but changed career and trained as a special needs assistant. She has worked in an amazing pre-school for the past two years and loves every minute of it.

How the Story Came About

This story all started with the title. Once I had that then the story just happened.

When I was training to become a special needs assistant I had a teacher who inspired me and ignited in me an interest in words and language. Then, when I began working as a pre-school assistant, I loved reading to the children and saw how much they enjoyed story time. They were so interested, inquisitive and transported to another world within the story. How brilliant is that?

I thought I'd love to help them do that, so I gave it a go and this is the result. Hope you enjoy it.

The Knight
Who Saved the Day

The Kingdom of Mayflower
was a beautiful place,
Ruled by King William
the Good and Queen Grace.
The sun shone so brightly,
the sky was so blue,
But something was different
and nobody knew.

Life here was lived
in a different way
Because DAY WAS NIGHT
and NIGHT WAS DAY!
When the sun came up
and daylight dawned
It was time for bed
and everyone yawned.

How strange to go to bed
when it's bright!
But the people of Mayflower
thought it quite right.
Curtains were pulled
and shutters closed tight,
Folks saying "Good day"
instead of "Goodnight".

238

They slept through the morning
and snored through the day,
They were comfy and cozy
in the beds where they lay.
The streets were deserted
with no one around,
The village was silent, there
wasn't a sound.

239

As the sun went down
and it began to get dark,
People were awakened
by the sound of the lark.
Everyone lit candles
to give them some light,
They had breakfast, lunch
and dinner at night.

The children at school
could not read their books,
The chefs in the palace
were unable to cook,
The ladies were sewing
but dropping a stitch,
The farmer and his sheep
ended up in a ditch.

The cows in the fields
were trying to see
As they bumped into each other,
the fence and the tree.
The birds were flying
but didn't know where,
Flapping all flustered
and lost in the air.

The King and the Queen
were beginning to worry,
They needed to come up
with a plan in a hurry.
"How can we help
and what shall we do?
You're bumping into me
and I'm bumping into you!"

King William the Good
was a generous man.
*"A Reward For the Person
Who Comes Up With a Plan!"*
He put up this sign
on the biggest oak tree
So the people of Mayflower
would pass by and see.

One morning the sun
was shining so bright
And into the village
arrived a young knight.
The name of this stranger
was Callum the Clever –
He was handsome and strong
and the smartest knight ever.

Callum the Clever
was puzzled and shocked –
There was no one in sight
and the doors were all locked.
Where were the villagers
on this beautiful day?
No one farming or shopping
or children at play!

As Callum was riding
his horse through the town
He noticed the sign
and took it straight down.
He galloped to the palace
and knocked on the door.
All were asleep
– he could hear them all snore.

He waited all day
until darkness fell,
Then the palace was awakened
by Callum's loud yell.
He called for King William
to tell him his plan.
The King was impressed
with this clever young man.

"Wow!" said the King.
"That's the best plan ever!
No wonder they call you
Callum the Clever!
'Sleep through the night,
stay awake through the day!'
It's a perfect plan!"
Everyone shouted, "HOORAY!"

If you enjoyed this book from Poolbeg why not visit our website:

www.poolbeg.com

and get another book delivered straight to your home or to a friend's home.

All books despatched within 24 hours.

POOLBEG

Why not join our mailing list at www.poolbeg.com and get some fantastic offers, competitions, author interviews and much more?

@PoolbegBooks